Seamus Ó Conaill

SPUDS
AND THE
CROCK
OF GOLD

ILLUSTRATED BY
Daniele Archimede

GILL BOOKS

It was the first of May, the start of summer, but for Spuds Potsofgold it was not a good day.

Two things had gone horribly wrong.

First, he'd been carrying his crock of gold back to Toadstool Cottage to polish it.

The sun had been so warm he thought he'd sit down and rest his back. Before he knew it, he was snoring away.

When he woke hours later, he jumped up and looked around.

'Shamrock shakes and chocolate cakes!
My crock of gold is gone!' he exclaimed.

Spuds ran back to Toadstool
Cottage, looking sourly at Bonnie
and Tyler, the two goldcrests who
lived in a chestnut tree in the garden.

'Shut up with that horrible singing!' he said.

But the birds continued to whistle their power ballad. 'What a grumpy auld grunchen.'

Spuds burst into the kitchen of Toadstool Cottage.
His wife, Rose Goodytwoshoes, and his pet mouse,
Steve, jumped. 'It's gone,' he wailed.
'I'm a pauper.'

'The crock can't have gone too far,' Rose said.
'You don't understand,' said Spuds.
'A leprechaun without his gold ... he might
as well be a troll.'

'Meow,' said Steve.
For Steve was convinced he
was really a cat.

Just then, the second
horrible thing happened.

Spuds's bulbous nose began to **quiver**, just a little at first.

Then the tip began to turn **pink**, then **red**.

His nostrils began to **wiggle** and **flare**.

Before he knew it, Spuds was inhaling deeply, the tingle in his nose like a thousand feathers.

'HHHHHAAAhhhhaAAAAhhhhaaaaaa ... CHOOOO!!!!!'

For it was the beginning of summer, and Steve had begun to moult his winter coat.

One of Steve's tickly little hairs had floated up Spuds's large nose.

The next morning, things were no better. Steve had been shedding lots and lots of tickly hairs overnight.

Spuds woke up with a giant sneeze. And another. Then another so violent that Steve jumped up and hid under a small chair in the corner of the room.

All around the bedroom were
millions of hairs. They were …

stuck
to the curtains

glued to the bed sheets

mashed into the carpet

But mostly they were stuck up poor Spuds's nose!

He and Rose got to work, dusting curtains,
shaking out sheets and cleaning carpets.
Bonnie and Tyler whistled a song to cheer
Spuds up as he grumbled and griped.

'What are you looking at?' he roared,
although he was interrupted by a sneeze.

Bonnie and Tyler jumped at the terrific
noise and flew away.

Finally, after cleaning up all the hairs, he was about to put them into the bin.

'Don't do that. Give them to me,' Rose said. She carefully took the clump of hair and put it safely in a little box.

'Things aren't always what they seem.
Treasure doesn't always gleam.'

Spuds gave a HUMPH. His crock
of gold had gleamed beautifully.

Over the next few weeks, Steve's moulting got worse and worse.

The hair got all over Spuds's smart green suit and hat. It stuck to the sofa and to the furry mat.

But the sneezes were what drove Spuds mad.
His morning paper always ended up with wet
splodges all over it, and one hhaaaachoooo
sent carrot soup flying across the kitchen.

Rose did her best to clean
all the hair she could,
putting it into a little box.

'Are you still carrying on
with that nonsense?' Spuds sighed.

Rose shook her head.

'Things aren't always what they seem.
Treasure doesn't always gleam.'

As the summer continued,
the sun got hotter and hotter.
Steve the mouse squeezed his eyes shut,
willing his hair not to fall out.

Spuds, his nose dripping and snuffling,
made all the wishes he could but the hair
still went everywhere.

Even Leggers McWeb, the
spider who lived in a crack
in the wall, decided to leave
Toadstool Cottage and visit
his sister in Dublin.

Rose, meanwhile, got on with things.

Whenever Spuds told her to throw out that 'dirty bundle' of hair, which was getting bigger and bigger, she said mysteriously,

'Things aren't always what they seem.
Treasure doesn't always gleam.'

Then autumn came, and just as the first leaves were starting to fall, Rose looked out the window.

'It's time,' she said, and she put the box out on the windowsill.

Bonnie and Tyler flew over, taking away little tufts of hair. After a while, some of their other bird friends appeared. Before Spuds knew it, the hair was gone.

'Hey,' Spuds called up into the chestnut tree. 'What do you want that itchy hair for?'

'For winter,' Bonnie said.

'In the snow, it'll keep us cosy, making our nests feel nice and toasty.'

'Thank you Rose, thank you Spuds,' they whistled.

Spuds thought about the two little birds flying from tree to tree. He called up,

'When you soared high in the sky,
did something shiny catch your eye?'

'We did see something very shiny in Maggie Magpie's nest,' Bonnie said. 'Gold coins in a bucket, or a basket …'

'A crock?' Spuds jumped with glee.

Spuds marched to Maggie
Magpie's tree and got back his
crock of gold, giving her a good
scolding. She was very, very sorry.

'It was a naughty thing to do,
but shiny things turn my brain
to goo!'

Every summer after that, when Steve would start to moult, Spuds would open his windows each morning and let Bonnie and Tyler fly into the house.

Within minutes, his curtains, clothes and sheets would be picked clean of the hairs.

In return, they'd whistle any song he liked and let him know if Maggie Magpie was nearby.

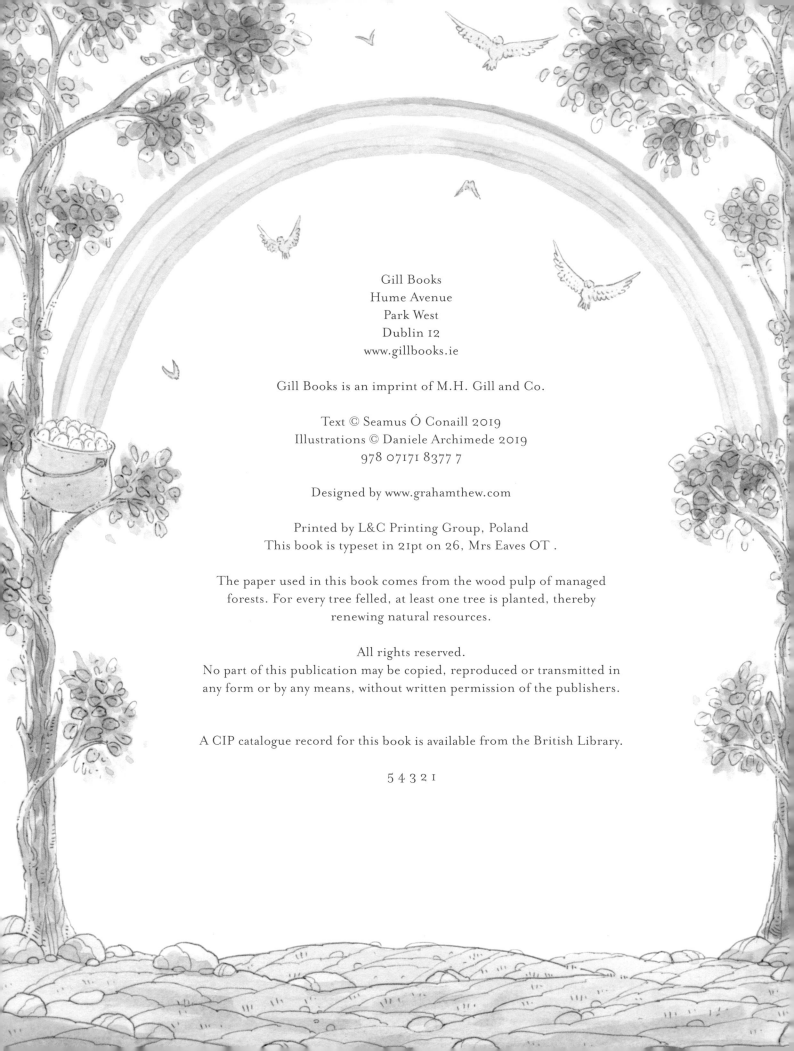

Gill Books
Hume Avenue
Park West
Dublin 12
www.gillbooks.ie

Gill Books is an imprint of M.H. Gill and Co.

978 07171 8377 7

Designed by www.grahamthew.com

Printed by L&C Printing Group, Poland
This book is typeset in 21pt on 26, Mrs Eaves OT .

The paper used in this book comes from the wood pulp of managed
forests. For every tree felled, at least one tree is planted, thereby
renewing natural resources.

A CIP catalogue record for this book is available from the British Library.

5 4 3 2 1